P9-EFI-840

Ten Little Christmas Presents

Presents →

Cartwheel ·B·O·O·K·S·®

SCHOLASTIC INC.

New York   Toronto   London   Auckland   Sydney
Mexico City   New Delhi   Hong Kong   Buenos Aires

Remembering Kristen Mary Faust 1978–2006

Library of Congress Cataloging-in-Publication Data

Marzollo, Jean.
Ten little Christmas presents / Jean Marzollo.
p. cm.
"Cartwheel books."
Summary: A counting-down book in which ten forest animals find
unexpected Christmas presents, left for them by a Secret Santa.
ISBN 0-545-02791-8
[1. Gifts--Fiction. 2. Christmas--Fiction. 3. Forest animals--Fiction.
4. Santa Claus--Fiction. 5. Counting. 6. Stories in rhyme.] I. Title.
II. Title: Ten little Christmas presents.

PZ8.3.M4194Aat 2008
[E]--dc22   2007021572

ISBN-13: 978-0-545-02791-5
ISBN-10: 0-545-02791-8

10 9 8 7 6 5 4 3 2 1   8 9 10 11 12/0

Printed in Singapore
First printing, October 2008

10 little Christmas presents, in snow so fine . . .

Mouse gets earmuffs! Now there are nine.

9 little presents—Owl can't wait . . .

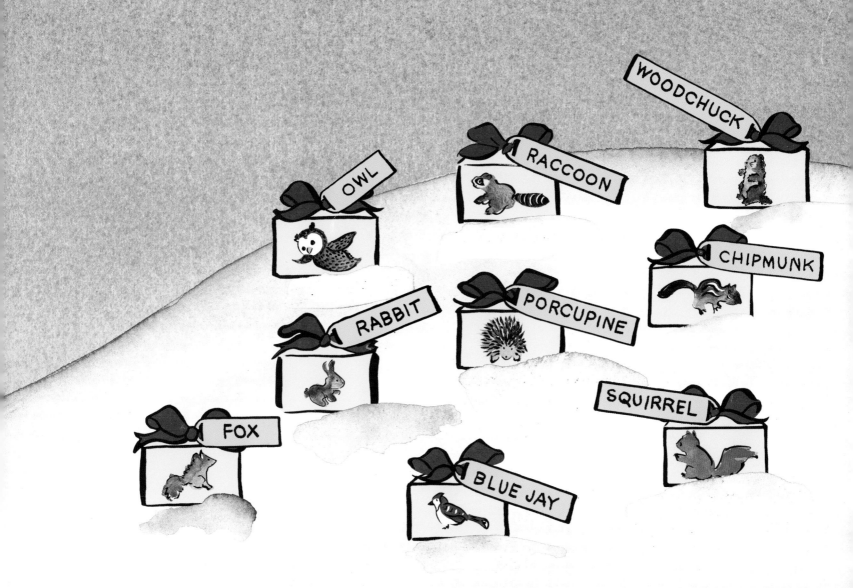

Owl gets a vest! Now there are eight.

8 little presents beneath a peaceful heaven . . .

Raccoon gets a scarf! Now there are seven.

7 little presents left in the mix . . .

Woodchuck gets a sweater! Now there are six.

6 little presents—the air feels alive . . .

Fox gets a poncho! Now there are five.

5 little presents on a snowy floor . . .

Rabbit gets a snowsuit! Now there are four.

4 little presents—what will they be?

Porcupine gets mittens! Now there are three.

3 little presents—each brand-new . . .

Chipmunk gets a jacket! Now there are two.

2 little presents—what a lot of fun!

Blue Jay gets a bonnet. Now there is one.

1 little present, the last gift of all . . .

Squirrel gets a tail warmer! And snow begins to fall.

Once there were ten presents.
Now there are none.
Whoever left the presents left one for everyone.

Who's our Secret Santa? The animals want to know.

"'Tis I," says Santa Bear.
"I was hiding in the snow!"

"Merry Christmas, everyone!"

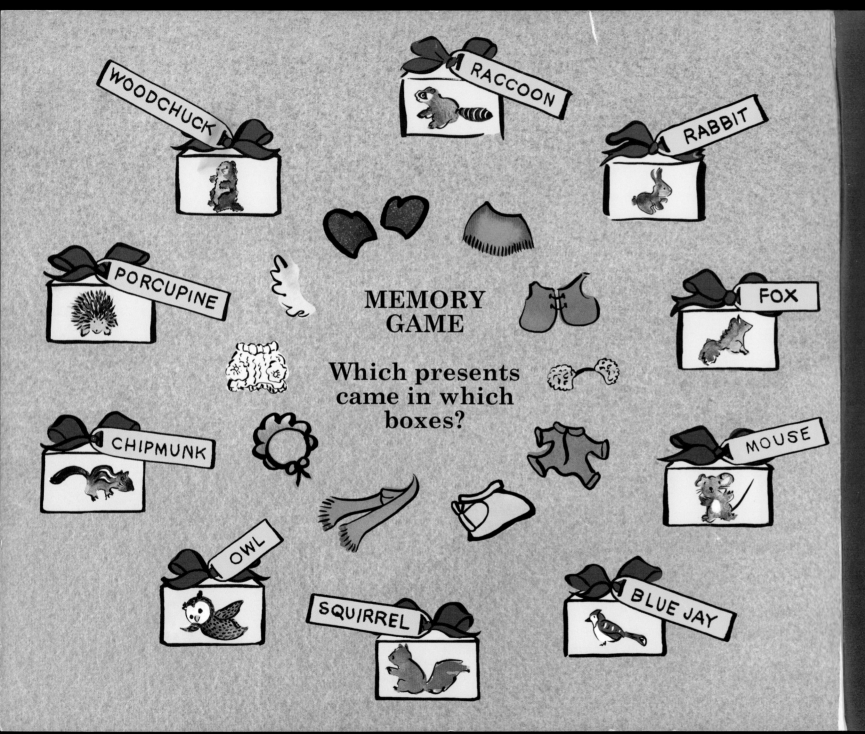

MEMORY GAME

Which presents came in which boxes?

WOODCHUCK

RACCOON

RABBIT

PORCUPINE

FOX

CHIPMUNK

MOUSE

OWL

SQUIRREL

BLUE JAY

"Merry Christmas, everyone!"

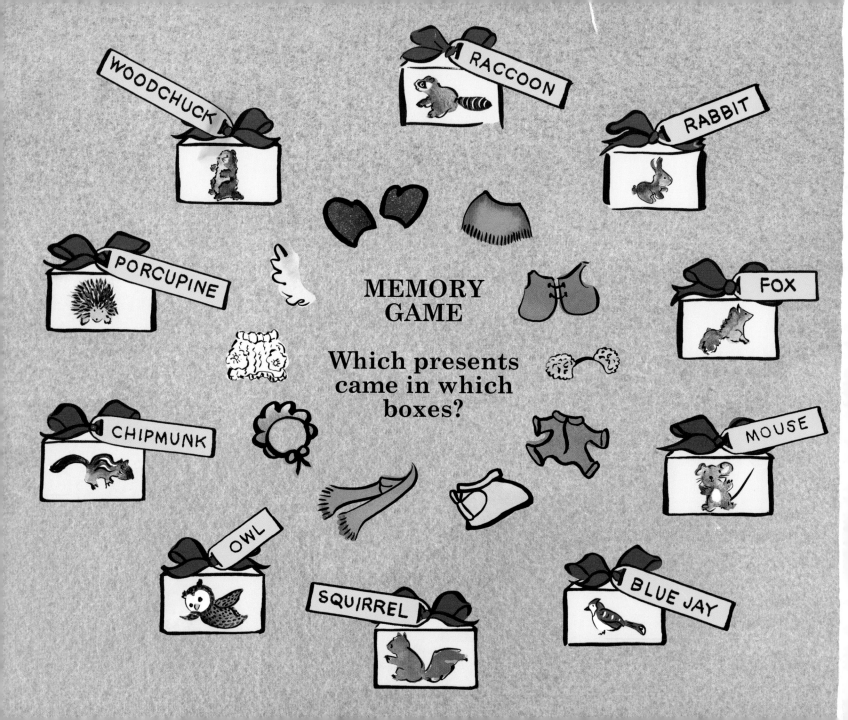

MEMORY
GAME

Which presents
came in which
boxes?